From a very young age, Daniele has always had a vivid imagination and been highly creative, splitting her time between music composition, writing stories, and pursuing her hobby of nature photography. She has a love of the outdoors, especially the Northwest Highlands of Scotland, where the peace and tranquillity serve to inspire and hone her creative thinking.

I dedicate this book to my dear parents for giving me such opportunity, filling my life with the joys of music, nature and culture, encouraging my creativity while being there for me, always. A special extra dedication also, to my wonderful Border Collie, Misty, for being my loyal and loving companion for many years in many walks.

Daniele Martin

THE GREEN SPIRAL

AUSTIN MACAULEY PUBLISHERS™

LONDON • CAMBRIDGE • NEW YORK • SHARJAH

A CIP catalogue record for this title is available from the British Library.

ISBN 9781398425897 (Paperback)
ISBN 9781398425903 (ePub e-book)

www.austinmacauley.com

First Published 2022
Austin Macauley Publishers Ltd®
1 Canada Square
Canary Wharf
London
E14 5AA

Don't read this story if you think that plants are blind, immobile, don't communicate, have no memory, and never sleep.

Part One

Chapter 1

The west coast of Scotland, sky overcast, windy.

Two teenagers, brother and sister, cycled to the end of a neglected, pothole-ridden road, close to the seashore. A rough track lay ahead, crossing peat bog and heather. They dismounted their bikes and laid them against a lichen-encrusted dry stone wall.

The girl pulled a small Moleskine® notebook from the inner pocket of her anorak and started to write.

"Sis, what do you keep scribbling in that book?"

"Oh, just ideas for a story Jamie," said the girl.

"What sort of story?" he asks.

"It's about an astrophysicist," she replied, hoping that would satisfy him.

"What does an Astrophysicist do?" he asked.

"They study the physics and chemistry of stars," she replied.

None the wiser, the boy just nodded and said, "Let's head for that rocky knoll over there. We'll get a good view of the sea."

Jude smiled to herself saying, "Great idea, perfect for taking some photos to show Mum and Dad."

A sea eagle soared above them, buffeted by a strong breeze.

They made their way across the pothole-ridden peat bog.

"See who gets wet feet first!" said Jude, in her hard-wearing walking boots, as she watched her brother stumbling and splodging his feet into the potholes, his trainers no match for her footwear.

They reached a heather-covered promontory and watched the grey green, white-topped waves crashing on the shore below. Jude sat down and started writing in her little story book, while Jamie, after emptying the brown peaty water from his trainers, took some photos of the waves, kelp covered rocks, and the flocks of fulmars diving through the spray.

Suddenly, the sky darkened. Jude noticed that Jamie had wandered further along the cliff edge.

"Jamie! Run! Run! Let's get back to the bikes, look what's heading our way, and fast!" Jude shouted, pointing to the black clouds rolling rapidly in their direction.

Lightning flashed, thunder rumbled, and it started to bucket with rain.

They ran back through the reeds and big clumps of heather, jumping from one soggy peat tussock to another. She glanced back to see where Jamie was, just as a bolt of lightning struck the very promontory they'd been standing on. Already soaked, they headed for a nearby wood.

"Lightning might strike the trees, Sis," said Jamie.

"Maybe, but it's more likely to hit the tallest, like that conifer over there," replied Jude.

They had taken shelter under a small tree with a dense canopy of narrow bright green leaves, resembling long soft pine needles. The trunk was smooth, unblemished, and sap green in colour. Jude was gazing up at the leaves. "I have no idea what kind of tree this is," she said.

Something very odd then happened.

The tree suddenly started to shed its leaves. The bluebells round the base of the trunk were soon covered.

"This is very weird, Jamie, none of the other trees are losing their leaves, and there's hardly a breeze now," said Jude, catching one of the leaves as it fell.

The leaf drop became a blizzard, spiralling wildly around them, like a mini-tornado. Suddenly it stopped, and the leaves all fell to the ground.

"Let's get out of here Jude, I don't like this," said Jamie.

Jude nodded, but her curiosity needed satisfying. "There must be a simple explanation, maybe a freak whirlwind, like when Dad was caught by a waterspout while sailing. Let's take a quick look in the wood first, to see if there are any more trees like this," said Jude.

"I'm not taking another step into this wood. Let's get out of here now," said Jamie.

Jude thought for a few beats then replied, "OK, give me a couple of minutes to have a quick look a short way into the wood, then we'll head back to the bikes."

"I don't like it Jude, but if you insist, just be quick. I'll wait here and take some pictures of this tree," Jamie replied.

Chapter 2

Jude strode off into the dark wood. She looked all around, but only saw conifers and elderly birch trees. No sign of any smooth, sap green barked trees.

She was just about to turn back when she sensed something behind her, the sound of the leaves rustling and twigs cracking. "Jamie! Is that you? Jamie?" No reply.

The sounds were getting closer, so close. Jude ran as fast as she could, heading deeper into the woods, lungs gasping, heart pounding, cannoning into small trees and stumbling over exposed roots.

She fell, arms outstretched, twisting and tumbling through the air.

Her head was spinning. She closed her eyes.

....

Jamie looked at his watch. Jude had been gone for nearly 20 minutes. He was worried but far too scared to venture into the woods.

"Jude! Jude!" he shouted.

No reply.

He shouted again and again. Still no reply.

So, though frightened, he took several sheepish steps among the trees, pulled out his mobile and tried to call his sister…No network coverage.

Next, for some reason, Jamie thought to look back through all the photos he'd taken earlier.

Strange. All the sea views were there, but not one single image of the green barked tree, they had all mysteriously disappeared.

He decided to retrace his steps, thinking to take further shots of the tree.

The tree was gone. Jamie didn't know what to do.

Chapter 3

Jude opened her eyes. She was lying on a padded bench, with a belt strapped loosely around her waist. There was a circular window to her side which made her think she was on board a ship.

"How on earth did I get here?" she asked herself.

Looking out of the port hole, Jude saw the moon, but not as she knew it. It was a weird orange blue colour.

She sat up and promptly bumped her head up against the rather low deck head.

"Oww!" she exclaimed, as she checked with her hand that her head was not bleeding.

Looking around the narrow cabin, there were doors at either end and numerous instrument dials. She was about to undo her seat belt when a whoosh came from one of the doors, and a man almost floated in, having to stoop on account of his tall stature. He was wearing a captain's naval uniform.

"Welcome aboard, young lady," he said.

"Where am I, and how did I get here?" Jude asked.

"You're on board the International Plantarium. I was only informed of your arrival a few minutes ago, and how you got here is also a mystery to me. My name's Robert, I'm the captain, and I believe you're Judith. Is that correct?"

Jude could not make any sense of what was happening. How did he know her name? Was this some sort of floating botanic garden?

"I'm usually called Jude, but how do you know my name? And how can I have landed on the deck of your ship? I was running through a woodland, not towards the sea," she said.

The captain thought for a moment, then said, "Firstly, let me explain what and where this ship actually is. This is a Space Plantarium."

Jude swallowed hard and her eyes widened.

"We are orbiting the moon, carrying plants with the hope of saving the most important resource on earth. Basically, we are doing what the story of 'Noah's Ark' didn't do," the captain explained.

Pointing to the port hole, Jude said, "So that's Planet Earth?"

"Not exactly Jude. You're here in a future time, and you're looking at a dying planet." He saw the total lack of understanding on her face. "We are like a lifeboat, carrying specimens of most plant species to have been discovered on Earth. Plant life on Earth is on a steep downward spiral if pollution, over-population and climate change cannot be reversed. I suppose we'll just have to start planting on Mars, or one of Jupiter's moons that have water," he said, with a wry smile. "I've been informed by Mission Control, who told me your name, that you are shortly to go to university to study Botany, and will be one of the many who will be key players in the battle to save plant life."

These words sent shockwaves through Jude. She had thought about a degree in botany, but still had several weeks of preparation for her final school exams.

"What! How would your Mission Control know such things?" she asked.

"The boffins there have clever ways of obtaining information. You've been sent here to learn about plants in a unique way, and to help others know plants as beings. If you and others don't succeed, Planet Earth will die. I'm sorry I can't be more helpful, but perhaps our two scientists, Francis and Sandy, whom you'll meet shortly, will have some ideas," said Robert.

The captain made his way over to one of the lockers, opened it and took out a wooden cabinet within which was a large hollow glass U-tube with side arms. Jude noticed the name inside, "Captain Robert Fitzroy RN.HMS Beagle."

"It that you?" she asked, knowing that the answer would confirm she must be dreaming.

"Yes, I took Francis's father to the Galapagos Islands. I've modified my barometer to predict the rate of atmospheric pollution."

A voice came over the tannoy. "Captain, Sir, Mission Control have reported a gas cloud on a trajectory that might cross ours."

The captain frowned saying, "I'll be on the bridge shortly." Then to Jude, he said, "Would you like to accompany me to the bridge, Jude?"

"I'd love to," she said, now just taking all the bizarre circumstances in her stride.

Chapter 4

Jude unbuckled her seat belt and assumed a nearly upright posture, steadying herself with the flat of her hand against the wall. She felt slightly queasy.

The captain obviously noticed her look and said, "You've had quite a bumpy journey to get here, and the weightlessness can take a while to get used to, so just take it easy and follow me."

They both floated their way along a tunnel-like passage lined with instrument panels and lockers labelled Drone Spares, Garden Tools, Fire Extinguishers, and Life Jackets.

Another surprise hit Jude as she floated onto the bridge behind the captain. There were five members of the crew, all seated in front of computer screens. The moment the captain entered, the five figures were instantly standing, and their heads all rotated 180 degrees to face their commanding officer.

Her first thought was that she was looking at life-sized versions of her brother's Lego® figures.

They all saluted and said in unison, "Welcome aboard Miss," with identical smiles.

Fitzroy saw the surprised look on Jude's face and said "We have a crew of seven robots altogether, five here on the bridge, MasterChef in the gallery, and Minty in the Plantarium. There are also drones with various robotic skills throughout the ship. Let me introduce the officers. Mandrake is our first officer, Number One, Magellan, navigating officer, Marconi, communications officer, Mustang, engineering officer, and last, but by no means least, we have Merlin, our security and environmental safety officer."

Merlin stepped forward and handed Jude a 'clip on' identity badge and said, "This will enable the drones patrolling the ship to identify you, should you wish to explore on your own, and if I may have your 'terrestrial' mobile for a moment, I'll install an app that enables communication anywhere on the ship."

Jude handed him her phone. He made some adjustments, then returned it to her. For some reason, Jude felt uneasy.

Addressing Mandrake, the captain said, "Can we have a look at this cloud you mentioned, Number One?"

"Yes, Sir," said Mandrake and nodded to Marconi. The image came up on the screen. Jude looked at the cloud. Black, blue, constantly changing shape, and within which Jude imagined she could see a pair of sinister-looking eyes.

Her mind flashed back to the thunder cloud that Jamie and herself had run from earlier that day.

"Do we know what its composition is, and does it pose a threat, Number One?" Fitzroy asked.

"Mission Control has identified gases similar to our atmosphere but with higher CO_2, and other chemicals so far unidentified. They don't think it poses a risk, Sir."

"Speed?" asked Fitzroy.

"Identical to ours, Sir, 26,000 kilometres per hour."

Jude's anxiety levels mounted, and Fitzroy sensed it and said, "We have very sophisticated defences Jude, and will pre-empt any problems by means of intelligence gathering. I will now introduce you to Joy, whom you have, in fact, already met. She is one of our Messenger trees."

Jude's eyes widened with curiosity and amazement when she heard that.

"A messenger tree, wow!" she exclaimed silently to herself.

Fitzroy nodded to Marconi, who promptly made a call over his intercom, and within seconds, the sap green barked tree, the very tree whose leaves had covered Jude and her brother earlier that day, appeared in front of her, as if from nowhere, with all her leaves intact.

"Don't ask me how she gets about or communicates, that science is way beyond me, but her messages always get results. Joy will drift through the cloud, picking up information," said the captain.

With these words, Joy was gone.

Jude wondered if Joy was some sort of virtual tree, and yet the leaves that had covered herself and Jamie earlier were real, or were they? Had they perhaps been in some kind of hypnotic state?

A sliding door opened at one side of the bridge, and bright sunshine flooded in from the Plant house.

"We'll go down the spiral staircase to meet our scientists now," said Fitzroy.

He nodded to Mandrake, saying, "You have the ship, Number One."

All five robots stood to attention and saluted.

Chapter 5

The staircase was densely entwined with numerous climbing plants and the air smelled of fresh leafy woodland.

"We're now going down fifty steps to the root house, where our scientists have their office and lab. The staircase certainly gives us good exercise!" said the captain.

Jude now had some idea of the vast size of the Plantarium.

As they descended, the woodland scent was replaced by a damp earthy smell.

Red lights illuminated the darkness. A door opened below them, and two men, wearing green lab coats, stepped onto a balcony.

The captain stood aside to let Jude pass.

"Welcome to the Root World, young lady," said one of them, a tall and slim, blond, bearded figure, dressed in green cords, and a light brown waistcoat over a floral shirt.

"I'm Francis, and this is my colleague, Sandy."

"Pleased to meet you, Judith," said the other scientist, with a broad Scots accent. He had ginger hair with wild eyebrows, and was dressed in tartan trews, white shirt, and donned a tartan bow tie.

Jude shook hands with them both.

"Come on in Judith, I've just made a fresh pot of green tea, and you can enjoy a slice of birthday cake, celebrating our 10 years in orbit. Don't worry about the captain and the rest of the crew, MasterChef has baked another cake especially for them," said Sandy, smiling at the captain.

As Jude stepped into the office, she wondered to herself how robots were able to eat birthday cake.

The captain told the scientists about the cloud and then said to Jude, "I'll leave you in their capable hands. I must now go and prepare for what might happen and await Joy's recon report. He nodded to the scientists and turned to ascend the spiral steps."

Meanwhile, in the officer's quarters, a drone was being programmed for spying.

The 'office' was in fact a lab, library, workshop, two bunk cabins, and kitchen-diner all rolled into one. Jude was given a perfectly fitting green lab coat and she went and sat down between the two scientists on a bench facing a large window with sliding doors.

Francis served out the tea and cake.

The cake was covered in green icing and was decorated with red berries dotted here and there.

"Pistachio and red currant chocolate cake. All the ingredients are grown here on board," said Francis.

Jude smiled, despite her dislike of pistachio nuts.

"Mmm, it looks wonderful!" she lied, taking a slice.

As she took a small bite, she caught a whiff of a familiar smell, but couldn't remember what.

Both of the scientists were enjoying large mouthfuls and seemed to be becoming more animated as they ate.

Sandy handed her a pair of sunglasses saying, "These are super smart specs. Francis and I developed them to help us understand plant behaviour and enable us to communicate with them."

He paused to observe Jude's reaction and smiled when he saw the look of amazement on her face.

"You mean you actually talk to the plants?" she said.

"Well, not exactly talk, though plants can detect and make sounds. We use vibrations to communicate. With the specs, you can see, hear and learn more about plant life. Something else that we cannot explain. When the Messenger tree is nearby, our thoughts can be transmitted to the plants. There are only three pairs of these glasses in existence and they are programmed only to function when used by Francis, yourself Jude, and me." Sandy explained.

Francis spotted the surprised look on Jude's face and said, "We acquired your 'specifications' from analysis of your physiognomy, your hobbies, especially your outdoor activities, and your recurrent dreams."

Now Jude's surprise turned to shock.

"How can you possibly know about my dreams?" she exclaimed.

Francis gently put his hand on her arm saying, "We are 15 years ahead of time on planet Earth. Remote mind-reading technology is now well developed, and AI can detect key recurring dream themes. Information technology has now almost eliminated confidentiality in every form of communication except the unmonitored spoken word. You might take comfort from the fact that Mission Control trawled through much of the teenage population of Scotland to 'find' you, and you must have impressed them with your subconscious thoughts about nature. Only someone clever enough to acquire knowledge of your neural pathways could use the Super Smart Specs to alter plants behaviour, whether that be for profit or other sinister practices. Human activity has already eliminated one-third of the natural world." he said.

These facts frightened her. She might become a target.

Sandy continued, "When you return to planet Earth, you will be able to teach others to understand and respect plants. Humans have regarded plants as materials despite us sharing half our DNA with them. They have not taken the time to look, listen and to learn how to be part of nature."

Sandy opened the sliding doors in front of the window and told Jude to put the specs on. She did so and gasped.

The spy drone hovered around outside the lab, transmitting all that was said. Ears on board and in an office at Mission Control back on Earth were listening.

Everything beyond the windows was clearly visible, bathed in a blue green light. Jude was fascinated at what was before her. She saw roots moving, heard strange sounds and could feel vibrations.

"You are looking at and sensing the way the root brain of this Oak tree works. All plants have their brains in their roots. Someone once said plants are like humans standing on their heads," said Francis.

The next surprise for Jude was a feeling that she was actually moving among the structures.

"Sandy, would you like to take over and give Jude a root tour?"

"Sandy's research has been in the fields of fungi and Penicillin," Francis added.

Sandy smiled and continued the commentary.

"With pleasure, Francis. Fungi used to be thought of as nature's means of dealing with dead tissue. In fact, they are essential for all kinds of plants. Plants have millions of root tips, and each one is like a data processing centre."

As Jude watched, she felt almost like she was a zoom camera.

"These specs are amazing, Sandy. What's going on over there? The roots all have fibres moving around them," she asked.

"These are fungi called mycorrhizae, essential for the health of plants and enable them to communicate. They form an underground web connecting all parts of a forest and beyond. We've been investigating the possibility of using the fungal web as a means of terrestrial communication. That could be important if, the already overloaded 'electronic highway' ever fails."

"Would you need the super specs to do that, Sandy?"

"We're working on that Jude. We think that the specs could possibly be modified to tap into the root web, a bit like a mobile, but this project is still off the record so keep it under your hat," said Sandy, winking at Jude. She nodded, smiling.

The 'ears' back at Mission Control picked up these remarks up with great interest.

"The mycorrhizae give plants essential minerals and growth factors in exchange for sugars made by the plant's leaves. The connections enable plants to help nourish sickly neighbours. The root brain senses sound vibrations, gravity and light levels. They breathe like leaves and are essential for deciduous trees during winter," said Sandy.

Jude began to realise how much there was to learn about plants.

"Do other creatures communicate with plants?" she asked.

Sandy smiled, and said, "Yes, there are many examples. Some plants under insect attack produce nectar that attracts insect eaters. Ants protect certain plants from predators in exchange for nutrition. Buzzing bees alert flowers to produce pollen which they can then carry to other flowers, in exchange for nectar. Some flowers create electric fields that attract bees. Ladybirds are rewarded for getting rid of green flies. Butterflies are drawn to flowers by patterns of UV light reflected off petals. I'm thinking your task will be to teach humans how to cooperate with plants."

Francis, standing at the other end of the window was focusing on a different part of the root network and Jude heard him murmuring to himself.

"He's talking to the roots," explained Sandy. "They pick up and interpret vibrations from his voice. Ultrasonic vibrations are detected and generated by tree roots, for example, if a plant has a water shortage, vibrations tell neighbouring plants to close stomata in their leaves. We are learning their language and have created a rough guide. I'll make a copy for you."

Francis looked across to them and said, "The trees are picking up toxin levels from their leaves, maybe there's been a breach in the hull's ventilation system. Why don't you introduce Jude to Minty and the plants on the upper deck and ask him to investigate? I'm going to discuss this with the captain."

Sandy nodded, went over to a photocopier, reproduced his 'Rough Guide to Plant Speak' and gave it to Jude, who popped it into the side pocket of her Moleskine®.

Francis called the captain and left.

Chapter 6

Jude and Sandy went up the 100 steps of the spiral staircase to the woodland. It was bright from the artificial sunlight and the air was refreshing, filled with woodland smells.

"No need for carbon dioxide scrubbers here," said Sandy.

"What are scrubbers?" Jude asked.

"Filters that absorb carbon dioxide. Without these in the rest of the ship, we humans would get CO_2 narcosis and perish. Merlin and his drones keep our atmosphere safe," said Sandy.

The next moment he was frowning, having noticed something was wrong. He went over to a Birch tree, pulled a stethoscope from his lab coat pocket, applied the bell to the tree trunk and listened. He frowned again, went to the neighbouring chestnut tree trunk and listened. Jude was fascinated.

"What were you listening for?" she asked.

"The murmur of fluid and bubbles of carbon dioxide moving up the trunk that occurs during sleep," said Sandy.

"So plants can make sounds like I was hearing from the oak tree roots?" said Jude.

"That's right Jude," replied Sandy. "All sound is vibration and it travels from roots up what's called the xylem, and down from leaves through cells called the phloem. Plants communicate with plants, insects and animals by sound, smell and touch. For example, the sound of leaves being chewed triggers messages to be sent to neighbours who will then produce unpleasant tasting chemicals. Gypsy moths eating leaves, or a bark beetle attack makes the plant release pheromones to warn others."

He pulled a branch of another nearby birch tree and moved several leaves. He then turned to Jude saying, "It looks like the trees are still in sleep mode. No one knows exactly how water can travel upwards when you consider some trees can be one hundred or more metres tall. Nature still keeps wonderful secrets. I also noticed that leaves on these trees are drooping just like flowers closing and stems bending at night. This means, that for some reason, there has been no response to blue daylight. Plants have structures you might describe as eyes in their green parts and they respond to blues and reds. I think something is messing with their root brains."

Jude had been aware of a blue haze throughout the woodland and asked what the cause could be.

"Well spotted Jude. That's an example of chemical messaging. Isoprene and terpene gases have been released. It is the trees reaction to a pollutant. Their leaves and needles trap polluting particles and release these protective chemicals, which the other plants detect with their superfine noses. When a plant is injured, ethylene gas is released. It has been described as the plant screaming to provide a warning to others that there is a threat nearby. These signs confirm what Francis suspected. Some pollutant has gained access. Let's ask Minty if he's checked all the vents," said Sandy.

The drone had followed Francis and passed a message to its controller.

Francis never reached the captain's cabin.

Chapter 7

Sandy used his mobile, and within seconds of the call, Minty came floating out of the woodland. He was quite different from the robot officers on the bridge. He was quite a bit shorter than they were, about Jude's height, and his head was less square, almost oval, and the exposure to open air and sunshine had given his face a slight tan and rosy cheeks. He looked like a Chinese schoolboy similar in age to her brother. Like the two scientists and Jude, he wore a green lab coat.

Minty introduced himself to Jude in a quiet voice, "Minty Ding at your service, Miss," then pre-empted Sandy's question saying, "All vents intact, atmospheric conditions normal but an unknown pollutant has been detected by our more sensitive plants, Sir."

He saluted Sandy who said, "Thank you, Minty, one jump ahead as always. Can we show the sensitive plants to Jude?"

"Certainly, Sir, just follow me," Minty replied.

As they followed the robot through the woodland, Sandy said, "Minty is highly intelligent, and for reasons we don't yet understand, he has a learning ability way beyond any other robot. He is the perfect plantsman. He loves all plants and his special interest is in seeds. His knowledge is encyclopaedic and far beyond what he was programmed to be. He knows every inch of this woodland."

As they walked among the trees, bushes, grasses, flowers, and lichen-covered rocks, Jude forgot she was on board a 'ship', in orbit around the moon. The woodland seemed vast, and she was aware of changing temperatures, humidity and scents as they proceeded deeper into the woods, and yet the woodland was continuous, not divided into separate climatic zones. Many of the entire range of plants, from tiny flowers to massive trees, she'd never seen before, not even in Edinburgh's Botanic Gardens. She then realised that every plant was moving, yet there was no wind.

"Sandy, the plants all seem to be moving, but there's not even a breeze. Is it the weightlessness?" asked Jude.

"You're certainly using your super-smart specs very well, Jude. All plants move in two ways. Leaves and flowers feed on light, so they turn towards the sun, and they all do a sort of slow spiral dance at differing rates unrelated to light or gravity, but so far, no one knows why. Minty will show you Mimosa's leaves reacting to being touched, and the Venus Fly Trap flowers closing when insects visit. Roots move towards food, and away from light, and there is one plant in our woodland that can even walk towards the light. It is called the Stilt Palm. It has roots above the ground which look like stilts. What it does is it allows the roots to die off when other nearby plants start to over shadow them and then sprouts new 'stilt roots' in the direction of light, so over time, the whole tree actually moves sideways," said Sandy.

Minty was examining a trunk up ahead when Jude caught sight of something fluttering between the bushes.

"Do you have butterflies in the woodland Sandy?" she asked.

The scientist looked around and said, "Oh yes, but it's still too early in our spring, so we haven't released any from the butterfly farm yet."

"But I've just seen a dark shape fluttering among these bushes over there," said Jude, pointing to some rhododendrons not yet in flower.

"We do have some nocturnal moths that help with pollination, but it's still a bit early in the season. Let's have a look," replied Sandy.

They both walked slowly towards the bushes. Sandy took a mini Dyson® like gadget from his lab coat. There was a dark butterfly shape on the soil beneath the bush. Sandy knelt down, switched on the gadget, and in an instant, the creature was trapped inside, fluttering frantically, with filaments hanging from its mouth.

"Gotcha!" shouted Sandy, "We'll soon see what this thing is. I'm sure it was removing mycorrhizae from the roots of the plant. It must have been a stowaway from when we left Earth."

Minty called them over to a lime tree and pointed to a crusty growth on the trunk, saying, "Lichen going into hibernation. More evidence of pollution."

Turning to Jude, Sandy frowned and said, "The questions are, what is it? And how did it gain access? Healthy lichens mean clean air. They consist of a fungus and an algae living together. The fungus protects, and the algae provide food from the sun. They grow very slowly and can live for centuries. A well-known motto applied to lichens is 'When the going gets tough, the tough shut down.'"

He pointed to several different lichens on the trees and rocks using descriptive names that brought a smile to Jude's face.

"Reindeer Moss, Red Coats, Babies' Molar Teeth, Blackberries and Custard, Witches Hair, and Goblin Lights, and there are many more throughout our woodland. I'm going to catch up with Francis and see what we can learn about this little creature. Minty will continue to introduce you to our, and now your, world of plants."

He left.

Jude now realised that she was being initiated into a new world and was being prepared for an unknown future. It felt quite scary.

Chapter 8

"Did you have some of that delicious birthday cake, Jude?" asked Minty.

The question caught Jude off guard. She thought for a moment, it definitely sounded like he'd eaten some.

"Yes Minty, it was delicious, did You…?" Jude asked, and broke her sentence, realizing she was asking a robot.

"My good friend MasterChef created it. Us robots have extremely fine-tuned olfactory function and we know how it must taste to humans," Minty replied.

"Minty, what do you think has caused the pollution?" asked Jude.

Minty looked at her with what seemed to be a sad expression, though his mechanical features did not really change.

"I am certain that the Black Cloud has been released from another spacecraft, with the aim of hijacking the plants. I think we are in great danger. Our plants are a priceless resource, and without the seeds, we have on board, the future of plant life, and therefore all life on the planet is very much in the balance," he replied.

Jude thought that, despite Minty being a robot, he seemed to understand the anxiety and uncertainty she felt. He talked in a quiet voice, almost as if she was telling Jude secrets about his family.

"Seeds are a miracle invention of nature, with benefits far exceeding any of man's invention. They contain the 'spark' of life that nourishes the baby plant, unites genes, travels, and endures. Some have germinated after centuries. I have collected seeds from all our plants and keep them preserved, safe, and ready to be ejected in a pod, should anything disastrous happen to the space station. Come, let me show you."

Chapter 9

Minty led Jude through the woodland to a clearing. A large flat stone lay in the centre of a sand-filled moat, in the shade of a very tall bamboo plant.

"I created this quicksand moat to protect the seeds," he said, and, taking a gentle hold of several of the bamboo canes added, "This was the fastest growing plant on Earth. She's called The Clumping Bamboo and can grow at a rate of up to two inches an hour when conditions are favourable. I've modified the seed to produce a plant that will grow ten times faster and can penetrate the hardest soil."

He took a handful of various sizes and colours of seeds from his lab coat pocket, rummaged among them, and handed a tiny one to Jude saying, "Here's that Bamboo seed. I never cease to be amazed at the energy released when a seed germinates."

The flat stone was covered with grey green squiggles that looked like hieroglyphics.

"What does that writing say?" asked Jude.

"Only mother nature can answer that. It's called Scripta lichen," said Minty.

He jumped over the moat, onto the stone and did a short tap dance type movement. The stone slowly rotated towards

Jude, making a bridge over the quicksand, revealing as it moved, an opening, with steps leading down.

"Follow me," said Minty.

Jude stepped onto the stone and followed Minty down the steps.

They descended into a root lined passage and after a while, they reached a silver egg-shaped object that was about twice the height of Jude.

It looked totally seamless, but when Minty whistled close to one area, a panel slid open to reveal a control panel, reclining seat, and there were numerous labelled drawers covering most of the interior.

"This is the space pod. It is situated next to the part of the hull which in programmed to automatically eject when conditions on board are critical," said Minty.

"Are there other pods like this on board?" Jude asked.

"I'm…." At that very moment, Misty's mobile rang. He answered immediately and listened for some minutes. Then said, "Yes Sir, right away."

He pressed a button on the control panel and, turning back to Jude said, "That was Sandy. Something terrible has happened to Joy, our senior messenger tree. She returned from her intelligence mission in the Black Cloud seriously injured and died in the captain's arms. Her bark had been stripped and some weird message had been carved on her trunk. The captain is distraught. Apparently, her last words were, "Black Cloud cold." The captain has given orders to alter course so that the ship will intercept and blast the Black Cloud with full power. Sandy said we need to prepare for extreme turbulence. He has asked me to introduce you to Jemma, Joy's assistant and sadly, now, her successor. She'll be your companion and ensure your safety during the uncertain time ahead."

With these words, Jemma was by Jude's side. Jude smiled and laid her hand on the slender, smooth green trunk, while looking up at Jemma's beautiful green, soft, needle-like leaves.

"She understands what you're thinking while you're wearing your super-smart specs, and you will also know what she thinks and suggests for you, whatever the circumstances," said Minty.

At that very moment, there was a loud roar from the ship's powerful engines, and the ship pitched and rolled as the captain set his plan in motion, to burn the Black Cloud. Jude had to steady herself, with the help of Jemma.

Chapter 10

Minty's head did a full 360-degree rotation, surveying the behaviour of the surrounding plants, then he took a carbon dioxide monitor from his lab coat pocket, examined it, and made a call on his mobile. No reply. Instead, a deep voice spoke over the tannoy, "Attention, this is Officer Merlin speaking. I am now in command. My fellow officers have been programmed to follow my orders."

At that statement, Minty shook his head, indicating that he had no intention of doing so.

The tannoy announcement continued, "Captain Fitzroy and the scientists Darwin and Fleming have been immobilised. The ship will be returned to its former speed and course." The tannoy cut off.

Despite the claim by Merlin that the engine power and course would change, the pitching and rolling seemed to be getting more violent, and the engine noise and vibration were increasing. The trees of the woodland looked like they were being hit by a tornado.

"Someone has switched off the carbon dioxide scrubbers, and almost certainly, Robert, Francis and Sandy are either unconscious or dead, from carbon dioxide narcosis. Thanks to the plants, we have been protected," said Minty.

The engine noise and increasing violence of movement suggested that the ship was out of control.

"Sandy had issued strict instructions for a situation where disaster threatened, that saving the seeds was a priority and when your arrival was announced, that you were to be equally prioritised."

Minty went up close to Jemma and put his head against her trunk. After a few moments he stood back, nodded, then turned to Jude and said, "Jemma will take you to a safe place until...." His words were drowned out by a siren.

Six drones appeared, along with MasterChef who was carrying a blow torch which he normally used for food preparation. He strode up to Minty, struck him across the face and, without warning, ignited the torch and blasted him.

Despite his lab coat bursting into flames, Minty lunged back at his assailant, ignoring the smoke and the flames. Three drones surrounded Minty in an effort to restrain him.

At that moment, Jude, still wearing her super-smart specs, 'felt' a message from Jemma, "Hide the S.S.S." Jude remembered Sandy's warning to prevent them from falling into evil hands and acknowledging the message with a nod of her head removed, the super smart specs and replaced them quickly, without being noticed, with her own sunglasses, pocketing the S.S.S.

"Take the girl and bring the specs to me!" shouted MasterChef, freeing himself from Minty's weakening grip.

Three drones immediately took hold of Jude. One drone snatched the sunglasses from her face and took them to MasterChef. A dark cloud appeared behind MasterChef. It consisted of many dark butterfly shapes, similar to the creature trapped by Sandy in the woodland. They began to attack Jemma, invading her beautiful leafy branches.

The violent movements and noises of the uncontrolled ship increased, and Jude lost her footing. The drones lost their grip on her arms. Minty, despite being consumed by the smoke and flames from his lab coat, and the 'synthetic skin' covering his mechanical and electronic structure being charred, struggled to escape from the mechanical arms of the drones. They overpowered him. Minty was now a smouldering, almost unrecognisable object. The all-metal drones, instructed by MasterChef, and unaffected by the smoke and flames, dragged him to the stone concealing the entrance to the seed and space lifeboat.

MasterChef, only lightly toasted, then demanded it is opened. Minty made no sound or movement. MasterChef wrenched a stout branch from a tree, stepped forward onto the quicksand and battered the stone. He started to sink, fell back and was swallowed down.

Jude watched with a mixture of horror and fascination. The drones continued to restrain her.

Chapter 11

An army of red ants whose colony had been violently disturbed by MasterChef, marched at speed out of the woodland and selectively over-ran Minty's and Jude's assailants on the ground, attacking them with venom and in overwhelming numbers. Jude herself was not touched by a single ant.

A loud buzzing sound ushered in a massive swarm of honeybees who immobilised the creatures attacking Jemma.

Their synthetic corpses fell to the ground.

Jude heard Jemma's voice telling her that she would take the super-smart specs, as there was yet another threat. Jemma was by her side for a few seconds, then was gone, with the specs.

The violent juddering movements of the ship continued, as did the engine roar. Jude went over to a nearby porthole and looked out. The ship, travelling at a phenomenal speed, was in the midst of the Black Cloud which was churning all around with flashes of lightning from within, striking the hull. Merlin had failed to take control of the ship's course and power. Robert Fitzroy had somehow locked the controls and despite him being either immobilised or killed, the Plantarium was still following his last command, to burn up the 'enemy.'

Jude was terrified.

For one moment, within the boiling cloud, she caught sight of a glistening black sphere. Minty had been right. Another spaceship had been controlling the Black Cloud! She looked to where Minty had been dragged by the drones. There were no signs of his burned, damaged body, nor his saviours, the ants.

A pair of chequered chef's trousered legs were protruding from the quicksand.

Chapter 12

The next threat arrived in the form of Merlin and more drones. The drones surrounded Jude and took her to the green spiral. Without letting her feet touch the steps, she was taken down to the bridge, through another passageway, into a space marked 'Sick Bay.' She was forced onto a CT scanner table and strapped down. Earphones were fitted and the scanning began.

Merlin was observing from behind a window.

He spoke, "The attention you have received would not have been necessary, and indeed, you would no longer be of any use to us if the scientists had not destroyed their Super Smart Specs. We shall eventually locate those given to you, and after calibrating parts of your prefrontal cortex, my Director will have the specifications required to be able to use them, and your usefulness will be at an end."

With these words, Jude thought of Jemma.

When the scan was completed, she was taken to a cubicle and locked in. The moment the door was locked, Jemma appeared and said, "It's time for us to leave the ship Jude, she has a very long journey ahead."

Jude was aware of a green spiral of leaves surrounding her, then she felt herself floating, completely relaxed, as if in a warm bath.

Chapter 13

Jude felt the leaves fall from her body and opened her eyes. She was standing in the woodland. No sign of Jemma the Messenger tree or her leaves. She then remembered that Jemma must still have the super-smart specs.

"So, what can I do?" she asked herself. Once again, she told herself it must have all been a dream. Even so, she'd learned many things about plants, and could tell others.

"Jamie! Jamie!" she called out.

Almost immediately came the reply, "Where are you, Sis?"

"I'm on my way!" Jude replied, walking in the direction of his voice. She saw him at the edge of the wood.

"Jamie, thanks for waiting," she said.

"Am I glad to see you, Jude, you've been gone for over 20 minutes? I thought you'd maybe forgotten I was waiting and gone straight back for your bike. What happened?"

"I tripped and must have been slightly concussed," replied Jude, having been prepared for that question, the true answer, she didn't even know herself. Had it all been a dream or hallucination?

"I'm sorry Jamie, thanks again for waiting. Let's go and get our bikes," she said.

The sky was bright now. A Skylark sang as it hovered above them.

Jude's mind was full of vivid images and voices as they walked back along the heather track. She noticed a shiny black Range Rover with a personalised number plate parked in a layby across from their bikes.

As they cycled back to the B&B, Jamie, who was in the lead, shouted back, "Remember that weird tree with the green bark? well, it disappeared, and when I looked on my mobile for the photos I'd taken of it, they were gone too! What do you make of that?"

Jude's eyes moistened as she recalled the images of Joy, who must have taken her on the journey, and given her own life in the struggle to save planet Earth's plant world.

"I'll tell you about it one day Jamie," she responded.

Jamie smiled to himself thinking, "She'll be putting that in her little story book I suppose."

Jude then remembered catching one of Joy's leaves after they had taken shelter under her canopy. She put her hand in her pocket. The leaf was still there, as was her copy of Sandy's 'Rough Guide to Plant Speak.' Now she was totally confused. She had not been dreaming after all.

The two teenagers cycled back to the village and finally arrived at the B&B just in time for afternoon tea. Jamie told their parents about the 'weird tree' but, at Jude's request, he didn't mention its disappearance or her 'concussion.' Their father agreed with the idea that the leaf drop had probably been a freak mini whirlwind, as he had experienced something similar while out sailing in the past. While the others were enjoying their teas, Jude excused herself, and cycled round to the National Trust Garden, hoping to find a tree resembling

Joy and Jemma. After exploring every corner of the garden, she failed to spot anything similar to tree or leaf. While cycling back to the village she decided to take Joy's leaf to the Royal Botanic Gardens and ask the tree expert if they could identify it, and suddenly remembering that it would soon be Jamie's birthday, she decided that she would buy some more Lego® for him, as he loved building all sorts of Lego® models.

She called the Botanic Garden office from the B&B to arrange a meeting.

That evening, an unexpected hailstorm crossed over Scotland.

Part Two

Chapter 14

The Admiral's suite, Her Majesty's Yacht, 'BRITANNIA', Port of Leith, Edinburgh.

"So, run that by me once more, Professor," said the man at the head of the long polished oak table. His gaze was bleak, and his voice seemed to come from somewhere beyond the room as if only an echo was being heard.

The Professor's response was hesitant. He was nervous, bordering on terrified. From what he had heard about the man facing him, any inaccurate, or incomplete information, and lack of absolute confidentiality would likely have life-threatening consequences for anyone consulted by this man.

Professor Andrew had been summoned to provide information.

"I have developed an agent that can be tailored to infect specific plants and the means whereby resistance to it can be applied when required. You'll be able to have immune plants when all others of the same species become affected," he stated.

There was a silence for several beats, then the echoing voice said, "How does this agent work? How is it transmitted? Do I have the entire stock? Is it already in my lab here on board?"

The professor was prepared for these questions with their implications and responded, "It prevents the plant absorbing water from the soil. It is spread by incorporation in plant feed, compost, topsoil, pest control sprays, seeds and seed packets, tree ties and stakes, and gardening gloves. It is resistant to drying, temperatures up to 50 degrees and down to minus 30 degrees. It is activated by contact with water. I have developed a handheld device that enables the agent to be introduced in seconds into any potted plant, growing shrub, or tree. A drone can be used to spray it on established trees and bushes. I have given the entire stock to your chief lab technician, and, as you instructed, have given my Swiss bank account number to your secretary."

"The funds will be transferred today," said the voice.

The professor felt a wave of relief tinged with apprehension at the thought of what he might have unleashed on the plant world.

"Thank you, Mr Neil," he said, rising from his chair.

The echoing voice called his secretary, "A meeting of the board will take place this evening. Those who cannot attend will be dismissed. Inform the lab to begin production of our acquisition, sufficient to target all garden centres, retail outlets selling plants and garden products, National Trust properties and Botanic Gardens."

That evening, the echoing voice sat at the head of the Admirals dining room table and silently surveyed the board members. His gaze was unnerving for everyone. No agenda had been provided for this emergency meeting. Without preamble, he said, "We can modify plants by spraying them with DNA, but it's hit and miss, and people object to us creating what they call 'Frankenstein' plants. This organisation will dominate all world plant business. Firstly, having sole ownership of a toxic infecting agent and disease-resistant plants, and secondly, I have knowledge of a device whereby we can modify plants by persuasion. We will be the world's sole owner. The device I shall obtain will enable this organisation to have control over the plant world, so we will dominate the food, drug and forestry industries. We have the most advanced and best-equipped mobile bio lab facilities here on board Britannia. I must have this device!" and with these words, he banged the table with his fist, causing every board member to physically jump. "I have reason to believe it is in the hands of a schoolgirl whom we are tracking through the GPS on her mobile phone."

Chapter 15

The family returned to Edinburgh.

The following day, Jude phoned the model shop to inquire as to whether they had a Lego® Space Station kit in stock. It was drizzling as Jude left their house, heading for the Royal Botanic Gardens. The tree expert had arranged to meet her in the library.

On arrival, she was informed that the dendrologist she had spoken to, had not come into work. Jude's sixth sense told her to be careful. She still heard Sandy's words regarding the Super Smart Specs, "In the wrong hands, they could lead to the extinction of more plants species." Could someone have intercepted her call to the tree specialist and now be tracking her in order to obtain the specs, though they could not know she didn't actually have them? She decided to make some observations on the people around her, thinking the best place to evade a stalker would be in the plant house where he or she would think concealment easy.

Jude knew the plant house very well from many visits since learning to walk and knew of one structure that would expose and test the skill of most. She smiled to herself thinking how appropriate that was after her experience in the Space Plantarium.

There would have to be two 'stalkers' in order to cover both entrance gates. She chose the west gate, figuring that the person would mingle with the customers browsing in the shop near the entrance. Jude spotted the individual, a female wearing a small backpack, and saw her use her mobile. Jude was sure that the second stalker would soon come into play.

She slowly meandered towards the large Victorian structure, all the while looking at trees and plants, and keeping an eye on her 'tail.' As she approached the entrance, she saw a large, steroid-enhanced, uniformed man enter, carrying two notice boards under one arm and guzzling bodybuilders drink. The female 'stalker' was standing looking at a rhododendron bush when a man approached her then headed towards the other end of the greenhouse complex.

Jude then realised she had three 'stalkers.' She opened the glass door and noticed a 'Closed for Cleaning' sign to one side. She glanced back through the glass door and saw the female hurrying to the entrance. When Jude turned round, she felt a knot in her stomach. Through the many climbing plants, she saw 'Uniform' slowly walking towards with a twisted smile on his face and rubbing his two exceptionally large hands together. The other 'Closed for Cleaning' sign had been placed at the doorway leading to the next section. She heard the woman come in and place the Cleaning sign at the main door.

It was now three against one.

Jude's reflexes took over. She took three long strides towards the approaching 'Uniform', who, for a moment, couldn't believe his luck. She then leapt over a chain onto the third step of the plant entangled Victorian spiral staircase, ignoring the "Do not use this stairway" sign, and bounded up the narrow steps two at a time to a cast iron balcony entwines with plants and overshadowed by tree and palm branches.

Jude had a plan in mind. She heard rather than saw, some activity and raised voices below. Halfway round the balcony, she pulled aside some palm branches to look down. 'Uniform' was jammed a few steps up the staircase and struggling to free himself, with the help of female stalker.

The woman who was obviously fit and strong, succeeded in dislodging him, then started up the steps, looking all around for Jude, who was concealed amid the plants.

For the first time in a long time, Jude felt the first wave of panic. What to do next? Should she try to climb down one of the palms? Phone the police? Give herself up? She decided, climbed up onto the balcony railing and reached for a stout branch. The next moment, she was pulled off the balcony railing by the powerful arms of the female stalker. Jude pushed back with both feet. The woman lost her balance and let go with one arm, enabling Jude to free herself from the other arm and stepped back, wondering what she should do next.

The answer came just as the woman was lifted off her feet and thrown over the railing. She fell backwards and landed on 'Uniform', who had been watching the action above while enjoying his 'power drink.' The women's backpack hit him in the face and chest. He fell, with the woman on top.

A container of the toxic agent, intended to infect designated zones in the Gardens, was shattered. 'Uniform's' sweet 'power' drink completed a cocktail extremely attractive to red ants. They swarmed from their colony in an aged tree trunk, attacked the humans, and neutralised the toxic bacterial agent with their own formic acid chemical weapon.

Jude looked at Jemma, and smiling, laid her hand on the smooth green trunk and said, "Thank you, again and again, Jemma. There are many questions I'd love to ask."

Jude felt, rather than heard, a message. "Things will become clear in time. I will know when I am needed." With that message, Jemma was gone.

Jude realised she had not asked Jemma for the Super Smart Specs, but then it dawned on her, she no longer needed them. Somehow, she was able to communicate with Jemma and other plants just by thinking, what was that called again? Then she remembered, when being restrained by MasterChef's drones, she'd thought, "If only I had the Super Smart Specs on, I could maybe summon help from the plants," and the ants had suddenly appeared! That's telepathy.

Angry shouting from below spurred Jude into action again and she lept onto a branch of the tree she'd planned to use to escape. She hit the ground running and was out the main door and immediately headed for the gate and her bike.

Chapter 16

Jude padlocked her bike to the lamp post outside 'wonderland models®' on Lothian Road. She was about to enter the shop when a personalised car number plate caught her eye. It was the same black Range Rover she'd seen in the seaside layby. Jude didn't believe in coincidence. Her 'alert button' had just been pressed. ERIN 50 M, an Irish reg? How would someone know she was coming to this shop? An image of her mobile being taken while on the Plantarium, came to mind. The pieces then fell into place.

She walked into the shop. It was alive with working models. Train sets running, Meccano® crane, bridge, engine and robot constructions, models of warships and planes, and kits for radio-controlled aircraft and drones. It felt like a time machine, which took the customer into the mechanical and electronic worlds of past, present and future.

There were no other customers in the shop. Jude went to the counter.

No assistant, and no bell or buzzer.

She waited for a few moments then said, "Hello, anybody there?"

No answer.

She noticed a box at the far end of the counter and went over. There was 'The International Space Station Lego® Kit,' with a 'Wonderland Models' card on top. She turned it over. In beautiful handwriting, the words, "With the compliments of Minty, for Jude. Please meet me this morning in the Chinese garden section of the Royal Botanic Gardens. Urgent." Jude was amazed, and had many questions that needed answers, but reacted instinctively. She picked up the kit and quickly left the shop. The kit went into her saddle bag and she headed for the Botanic Garden.

Chapter 17

Jude left her bike in the Botanic Gardens' east gate cycle stand and hurried to the Chinese garden. The constant drizzle had kept visitors at home. Banks of mist floated around the trees and plants. She did not encounter anyone and walked up the steep, winding muddy path among all the oriental plants. A stream almost in spate from several days of rain poured down from the top of the slope on which the garden had been created. Tall bamboos overhung the path.

"Minty, Minty!" she shouted, to be heard above the noisy rushing stream.

The path became steeper and obscured by mist.

Jude heard a faint voice coming from within a group of rhododendrons, under an overhanging Weeping Willow tree. "I'm here, Jude," the voice replied.

Jude pulled aside a few branches and was shocked at what she saw. Minty was almost unrecognisable. The remains of his charred green lab coat were fused with the twisted, deformed, melted synthetic skin that covered the robotic skeleton. His boyish Chinese face was now a blackened, wrinkled mask. His quiet voice was as Jude remembered it.

"We don't have much time, Jude," he said. "I sense the approach of those who mean to do us harm. Your mobile has been leaking your location since that evil Merlin installed his app. You must go in a few moments."

"You mean he is here now Minty?" asked Jude.

"No, his Controller is. He's called Neil, the evil character behind the scheme to control the plant world. Merlin is now either floating endlessly in space or is robotic debris on one of Jupiter's moons. Captain Fitzroy somehow managed to regain control of the Plantarium, before succumbing to carbon dioxide narcosis, and set course for Jupiter. I was able to escape in the Seed Pod and reach planet Earth. I have left all the seeds here in the garden, in a secure place you are familiar with, and came to this Chinese garden, the nearest I'll ever be to China before my time runs out. Remember the Green Spiral," he said.

He then rotated his head 360 degrees and added, "They're coming up the path. Do you still have the special bamboo seed I gave you?"

Jude put her hand in her pocket, produced the single seed and handed it to him.

"We'll meet again each time any of the seeds I have collected germinates."

Moments later, from two separate directions, four figures emerged from the mist. Jude recognised two of them from earlier, the female stalker, and the steroid junkie, whose face was covered in boils and red swellings, thanks to the ants.

The female was pushing a large empty pram. Jude didn't connect any dots at this point.

They both took a hold of Jude and roughly forced her onto her knees. The woman then searched Jude's anorak and jeans, then shook her head saying, "Negative, Mr Neil."

A second man pushed Minty over onto his side and stamped on his head with what looked like size 15 muddy Doc Marten® boots. The one called Neil was tall with broad shoulders, and shiny black hair could be seen extending down his neck, under a white broad-brimmed hat. He had a pale, expressionless face that looked as if it had been sculpted from marble and wore dark glasses despite the gloom. He was wearing a long white raincoat.

He looked at Jude and bellowed with a deep voice that sounded like an echo from somewhere distant, "Where are the Super Smart Spectacles?"

"I don't have them," said Jude.

"If you don't wish to become another 'never to be found' missing schoolgirl, you had better tell me where they are, and to help you answer that correctly, you can now watch the deconstruction of a robot. I shall delay removal of the vocal functions, so you can enjoy the sounds of a distressed, highly intelligent machine, who is not devoid of emotion," said Neil.

Jude now knew the purpose of the pram.

Neil nodded to 'Doc Martens', who proceeded to pull off pieces of Minty's outer shell. Minty, lying on his side facing away from the others, used his one free arm to remove a handful of muddy soil, plant the Clumping Bamboo seed, then, with a mighty effort, he rolled towards 'Doc Marten', toppling him onto the pram, which in turn rolled onto the woman and the steroid junkie, who then dominoed into Neil.

"Run! Jude, run!" shouted Minty.

Jude lept to grasp a willow branch, swung over their struggling bodies and sprinted down the path, now under running water. As she powered downhill, there were shouts from behind. She glanced back to see another amazing example of plant behaviour. The fastest-growing plant in the world was breaking all records, thanks to Minty's 'enhancements.' The pram, writhing bodies, arms and legs, were entangled in a moving web of bamboo branches. Jude still had Minty's last words in mind as she ran back to her bike at the east gate.

That night, a figure crept onto HMY Britannia, entered the laboratory, and destroyed the entire stock of the bacterial agent.

The following day, there were three strange news items.

An incident involving tree branches is being investigated at the Royal Botanic Gardens, Edinburgh.

A large donation has been given to Royal Botanic Gardens by an anonymous donor.

Vegetation has been identified on one of Jupiter's moons.

When Jude heard that last news item, she knew Robert, Francis and Sandy must have been planting, and, recalling Minty's last words, knew where he had left the seeds. She would ensure he would never be forgotten.

Jude decided that provided she did well in her exams, she would apply for the Botany course at university, and not medicine as her father had hoped.

She took the beautiful Messenger tree leaf and 'The Rough Guide to Plant Speak' from her anorak pocket and started to write in her Moleskine® book.

"Would anyone actually believe her story?" Jude asked herself.

Part Three

Chapter 18

Svalbard, the Nordic word for cold coast, is an archipelago between Norway and the North Pole. The average temperature is -8 degrees C falling to -50 degrees C. The Permafrost and ice in this area has been up to 800 metres thick for centuries. Recently, however, with temperatures reaching all-time highs of over 21 degrees C, this icy layer is thinning rapidly.

The World seed bank was created on Svalbard, inside a permafrost covered sandstone mountain. This seed collection is now under threat from global warnings.

....

Early morning, late spring, the West Sands, St. Andrews. A blue sky, wisps of cloud, seagulls hovering almost motionless in a slight breeze. The tide is far out.

Two women, dressed in figure-hugging track suits, jogged at an easy pace along the shoreline, unaware that they were under observation.

Jude, near the end of her first year of a Botany course, was accompanying Dr Susan Woodside, the Senior Lecturer in the Department of Plant Intelligence, on a two-mile run. This had become a weekly event providing exercise in a spectacular setting and an opportunity to discuss Jude's research. Jude had never revealed the source of her knowledge about plant behaviour that had so impressed her running companion. This morning they were discussing Prof Andrew's trip to Switzerland to present a research paper at a scientific meeting.

The idea behind the research had come from a chance observation made by Jude. The two lab technicians, Frank and Alec, played Scottish country dance tunes on fiddle and accordion in the lab before locking up at the end of the day. Jude's research involved studying plant growth and she noticed a marked difference in the growth rate of both seedlings and tree saplings between those in the 'musical lab' and similar plants in the one next door. Jude remembered well, the look of amazement on Susan's face when she brought this to her attention.

"That is fascinating, Jude. Any explanation?" said Susan.

"Well this might sound crazy, but the plants seem to have benefited from music," replied Jude.

Susan had stopped in her tracks causing Jude to do the same. "You know, Charles Darwin thought that mimosa leaves would respond to his bassoon playing, but nothing happened, so he called it a foolish experiment. Since then, no one has proven that plants can hear, although they can sense vibration and have genes associated with deafness in humans. Jude, you may just have revived Darwin's hypothesis," she said.

In the months thereafter, a small preliminary study had been undertaken and in view of a French study showing that plant growth is affected by radio waves, the research paper was accepted.

Chapter 19

The Lake of Zurich.

The blast of "Stadt Zurich's" horn announced the ferry's departure from Wolishaven's harbour. The sky and choppy lake were leaden grey. The ferry to Zurich central harbour was crowded with commuters heading for businesses and offices. Professor Andrew managed to find a seat in the restaurant and ordered croissants and cappuccino. The botanist had spent an enjoyable evening and night with an ex-colleague. They had shared a fondue and delicious mixed salad accompanied by a dry Saint Saphoran wine and followed by her own very special apple strudel and cream. He smiled to himself.

He opened his bright green leather briefcase and took out the paper he was about to present to the world's top botanists. In addition, he had been honoured to receive an invitation to join an international working group planning a rescue mission involving the creation of a Space Plantarium that would orbit the moon. He gave a sigh of relief that the plant toxin project had been stopped and Mr Neil's money returned. His donation to the Royal Botanic Garden, though costing him dearly, had eased his conscience.

The "Stadt Zurich" docked at the central harbour. Wind and rain welcomed the passengers as they disembarked. The bright green leather briefcase was being carried in one black leather gloved hand by a tall man wearing a long white raincoat. He had broad shoulders and shiny black hair extending down his neck under a white, broad-brimmed hat which he held with his other gloved hand.

Professor Andrew was not among the passengers who disembarked.

Chapter 20

St. Andrews.

The mysterious disappearance of Professor Andrew was felt by most academics to be a tragic loss to the University.

Prof J.D.H. Kelly, Head of Bioengineering, Robotics and A.I., thought it was a timely opportunity to 'inject new blood into a 'tired' Faculty of Botany. He openly declared he had little time for plants.

"Machines are the only way to ensure the survival of the human species." Yet when invited to develop robots and drones for the International Plantarium, he grasped the opportunity. He had hidden motives for becoming involved.

The seed crisis deepened as climate change and the human destruction of the natural world-advanced. Seed merchants, stock market dealers, criminal organisations and certain governments 'bought up' the market.

There was, however, still one source of world seeds beyond the reach of criminality. Minty's collection. Jude had been unable to locate it. He had specifically used the description 'Green Spiral' in relation to its location in the Botanic Garden.

Jude decided to tell the whole story to Susan. Perhaps if they could find the remnants of Minty, she might be able to extract information from the microchips. But that 'techno stuff' was beyond her.

Susan had been appointed acting Head of the Faculty of Botany and had received a telephone call from Kelly, urging her to collaborate with him on projects. His voice and language made her feel a little uncomfortable. He then asked her to help him programme a Botanic Robot or "Bot Bot" as he called it.

"Perhaps you could join me at my residence one evening to discuss the requirements since I'm sure like me, your days are taken up with teaching," Kelly suggested.

She agreed to a meeting at his residence. The prospect made her cringe, but to ensure proper input, she decided to grin and bear it.

Chapter 21

On arriving at Kelly's house, situated on The Scores, a road with a magnificent view to the sea, the door was opened by an athletic-looking female. Kelly appeared in the doorway of a large room behind her. He had a dark, narrow, expressionless face, a hard stare, and black bushy eyebrows in contrast to his completely bald, pale pink scalp. He was tall and advanced to meet Susan with a limp and using a walking stick. A stand in the hallway carried several walking sticks, all with differing, ornate handles.

At that first 'face to face' meeting, in a rather high-pitched voice, his opening remark set 'alarm bells' ringing in Susan's head.

"Tell me about this student of yours who has some sort of ability to communicate with plants."

Susan had not been aware of any such thing but in a flash remembered Jude once talking about understanding what plants could teach us. Susan found it worrying that he, who worked in a totally different faculty, situated at the other end of St. Andrews, should know detail such as this about a first-year student. Susan said she had no knowledge of that claim and quickly turned the conversation to robots. He did not look satisfied with that response but turned to his favourite project.

"I have been asked to create seven robots, which I've called my M series, the 13th robotic design I've made. They are all named after some historical or celebrity character, Merlin, Mandrake, Magellan, Marconi, Mustang, MasterChef and what would you like to call your Bot bot, Susan?"

Susan was caught off balance by the question but even more by Kelly's use of her first name. She thought of the name of a celebrity gardener and said, "How about Minty Ding?"

Kelly smiled saying, "Amusing, a Chinese Bot bot." Then something surprising happened. Kelly repeated the same phrase "Amusing, a Chinese Bot bot," repeatedly with a blank look on his face. He then blinked several times, walked to the lounge door, opened it and called on the 'athletic' woman to show Susan out.

As Susan stepped out into the cool moonlit street, a shiver of fear ran through her. She decided she must speak with Jude at once and set off towards Baker Lane where Jude shared a flat. Within five minutes she was aware of being followed and headed for assistance. She caught the aroma of her destination about fifty yards away, as she turned on to Market Street.

The brightly lit 'Fitz for Fish and Chips,' was overflowing with student customers waiting or eating. Bob Fitzsimmons spotted Susan through the window and ploughed his way through his customers. He was a large man in every respect with a weather-beaten face from the North Sea winds he was constantly exposed to while hauling in his catch every day from the deck of his fishing boat.

He gave Susan a gentle 'bear hug' saying, "You look worried Sue. Need help?"

"Yes Bob, I think I'm being stalked. Can I go out the back door?" Susan asked.

"No problem," he said, clearing the way through the hungry customers and picking up a fish supper from his daughter who, along with her brother, was frying and serving.

"Your favourite, on the house, and I'll 'persuade' your stalker to find another hobby," he said with a twinkling eye and a booming voice.

Chapter 22

Susan reached Jude's flat in the narrow Baker Lane.

After sharing the fish supper, she told Jude about Kelly's interest in some story that Jude was able to communicate with plants. On hearing that, Jude 'launched' into her story with every detail she could remember. She gave Susan the Plant Speak vocabulary. Susan was silent and listened with an astonished look on her face.

Jude finished her story then said, "Do you think these things could actually have happened?"

Susan remained speechless for a moment, then it was her turn to drop a bombshell.

"Jude, you won't believe this, but I will be programming a robot I named Minty Ding! Exactly as you described in your extraordinary journey! Now I don't believe in coincidences. What made me choose that name? If there is no rational explanation then, to paraphrase Sherlock Holmes' words, no matter how extraordinary, the answer is the robot told me! I will be working on, what appears to be an old generation and very battered model. You describe Minty as being severely damaged and burned. There were no signs of burning on my robot. I was given the chance to view the robot the day before Kelly's invitation, by one of the robotics technicians. Perhaps then, Minty 'implanted' his name in my mind. And there is something else. I was invited to examine that extraordinary superfast growing Clumping Bamboo after the incident in the Botanic Garden. I spoke to the gardeners who were on the scene shortly after it happened in the Chinese garden. They said there were two men and one woman. An empty pram was squashed almost beyond recognition but no robot. I spotted a strange conifer close to the bamboo which I could not identify so I took a leaf, which I still have."

At this point, she opened her diary just as Jude removed her Messenger tree leaf from her Moleskine® notebook saying "Snap!"

Susan gasped and said, "You mean this leaf that I have, has come from the Messenger tree, Jemma, who protected you during your extra-terrestrial journey?"

She then added, "Oh, and perhaps to confirm the concept of an extra-terrestrial event, I returned to the Chinese garden the next day and the tree had gone!"

"That must have been Jemma and she has transported my Minty to ….," Jude thought for a moment then continued, "Your Minty and mine are one and the same and Jemma has disguised him to resemble an old relic, so he will already be programmed botanically."

Susan said, "We'll soon find out Jude. Let's go to the lab now. Kelly's technician has given me a passkey for the lab, so we can slip in tonight and see if you recognise him, Oh, and incidentally Jude, on my way here I was stalked, so we both need to be on our guard. Minty's cache of seeds and your plant communication skills are strong motives for serious crime."

"And if you really have Minty, he can tell us where the seeds are hidden," continued Jude.

"One more thing Jude. I'm going to ask a dear friend of mine to teach you a couple of 'tricks' to have up your sleeve should any of our adversaries threaten you. Ever heard of Dim-Mak?" said Susan.

On entering the lab, the moment Jude saw Minty, a voice in her head said, "Yes, it's me, Jude." She smiled and just nodded.

Chapter 23

Susan was given a free hand to programme the 'Bot bot' as she thought appropriate though Kelly kept dropping in with ulterior motives that had nothing to do with robotics, usually when the two lab techs were on a break. They were friends of Alex and Frank, the botany techs, and were not 'fans' of Prof Kelly. They told Susan that Kelly had instructed them to provide her with a 'used-derelict' structure from one of the early 'series.' The robot they uncovered under a heap of outdated and degraded electronic and mechanical equipment was truly dilapidated, neither of the techs could remember having seen it in action.

With their ingenuity and repair skills, Susan set to work programming her robot. As Jude had confirmed, he was, in fact, the original Minty brought from the assault in the Botanic Garden by Neil and his lackies. His incredible botanic brain was still intact. Susan provided 'him' with certain additional skills that Kelly would not know about.

Chapter 24

Jude and Susan had coffee in Costa's on Market Street.

"Tonight, when Kelly's left the lab, we'll take Minty to the Royal Botanic Garden in Edinburgh and ask him to show us the Green Spiral of seeds. I have a pass key which I was given to allow me access to the library and garden. Incidentally, how did you get on with Madam Yang at her acupuncture clinic?" said Susan.

"Fantastic. She's a remarkable woman. I had never heard of Dim-Mak. It's quite scary stuff. And she has a phenomenal knowledge of herbs, plant remedies and toxins. I think my father would be impressed with the knowledge of human surface anatomy and the nervous system that I've learned from her." said Jude.

"Excellent Jude. I feel easier knowing that. I'll pick you up at 8 pm this evening," said Susan as they left the café.

Chapter 25

Midnight. Full moon. A cloudless sky.

Minty led the way through Edinburgh's Royal Botanic Garden. They were spotted on CCTV by the security team. They recognised Susan and her student, Jude, from previous visits and knew that her research often involved the study of nocturnal pollination by moths.

Minty led them to an area of native species, called 'Wild Woodland.' He stopped in front of a large, mature poplar tree entwined in a dense spiral of ivy. Around the base of the tree, there were several young poplars with straight stout stems.

"Remember the heavy hailstorm last spring. It was just at the end of your Highland holiday, Jude. Snowball sized hailstones containing seed pods fell onto this tree. Very accurate 'bomb' aiming on my part. She's your green spiral, Jude. Leonardo Da Vinci called it Nature's favoured form," said Minty pointing to the curving ivy stem.

Susan was smiling. "I don't know why I didn't think of that when we puzzled over the Green Spiral's location yesterday, Jude. There are more climbing plants than those with a single stem. Light is food for plants so they 'hitch a ride' up to the light and do not need to wait for years to gain height. And even more fascinating Jude, this could be the oldest tree in Scotland. We have here, an example of what some might call 'immortality.' The tree sprouts genetically identical saplings sharing the same parent roots. One popular in the USA, known to be 130 years old, had sprouted from roots dated as 80,000 years old," said Susan.

A boiling black cloud appeared as if from nowhere. Jude immediately recognised it as the cloud she had seen from the Space Plantarium. It was the same cloud which Joy, the senior Messenger tree, had been sent to investigate by the captain, and from which she had returned with a fatally injured trunk. The cloud seemed to hover over the 'Wild Woodland.' Jude turned on hearing the rustle of leaves.

Chapter 26

Kelly, Neil, the athletic-looking female and the 'steroid junky' appeared in a line facing the three. Kelly spoke.

"Four prizes all for the taking. The girl with the plant secrets, the hoard of seeds, which I assume are concealed here, a fully functional Bot bot and…," Kelly paused to relish the thoughts he had, "A colleague who will show me hidden talents."

He had his walking stick in one hand and, with the other twisted the handle and pulled a rapier from inside the hollow stick.

He advanced towards Susan directing the point of his sword at her throat. At the same time, Neil stepped towards Jude, raising his gloved hands, while the large fat man, followed by the athletic woman, came from behind.

Minty, by Susan's side, must have read her thoughts. Ever the supreme gardener, he produced a large pair of secateurs from within his arm structure, cut through the stem of a stout sapling, and handed a one metre length weapon to Susan.

None of the onlookers were prepared for what happened next. Susan, captain of the university fencing team, went 'on guard.' Kelly smiled for a few beats, then Susan parried the rapier and, with feral ferocity, lunged at his chest.

His expression changed from surprise to fear and then to anger. He staggered, made a muffled grunt of pain, and then shouted, "I will show you no mercy, Miss Woodside. Your fate is sealed."

He leapt forward, aiming his sword towards Susan's chest, demonstrating an agility that belied the need for a walking stick. Susan parried the lunge, which ripped her jacket and followed through aiming her sapling at his neck. It made contact with the skin of his cheek which then shredded.

She had pierced a mask. At that moment, Minty switched on one of the secret weapons Susan had installed. An intensely bright, flickering strobe light was directed at Kelly's eyes. He immediately had a Grand Mal epileptic fit. Neil let go of his vice-like grip on Jude's arm and rushed to catch Kelly who was in the act of falling while he convulsed.

Minty raised an arm and it extended with the secateurs directed at the main stem of the climbing Green Spiral of ivy. A huge, mass of leaves, branches and stem, containing hundreds of heavy snowball sized seed capsules, tumbled down on top of Neil and Kelly, completely covering them. There was no possibility of movement under such a weight of plants.

The fat man followed closely by the woman stepped towards Jude to be met with a Dim-Mak back fist strike to one of his eyeballs. He immediately blacked out and fell backwards onto the woman who let out a screech as her chest was squashed.

There was a rumble from the hovering cloud. Jude looked up and saw Jemma appear to one side of the huge poplar. Then, as if light as a feather, Joy, her bark healed, floated down from the cloud and spontaneously merged with Jemma, to form one tree the size of both Messengers combined.

This new single tree looked as if it had been growing there for many years.

The black cloud seemed to melt away, and, for a moment, a thought crossed Jude's mind, "Perhaps the cloud had been delivering a warning message from life elsewhere."

Chapter 27

The security guards with two police officers arrived in a tractor drawn trailer. They arrested the still groggy, steroid junky and the rather wheezy athletic woman.

The massive pile of 'snowballs' and ivy that had buried and crushed Kelly and Neil took some time to load onto the trailer. The two men were lying face down, alive but unconscious. When the policemen turned them over, Kelly's mask had gone. Kelly and Neil were identical twins.

The twins recovered consciousness in hospital under police guard. The neurologists thought that Kelly had permanent retrograde amnesia as a result of the epileptic fit. He would never return to his academic post. A search of his house revealed the bright green leather briefcase that Prof Andrew had taken with him to Switzerland. Although charges were made against him, the case against Kelly was not proven. He was to spend his remaining years in an 'Institution.'

Neil somehow managed to avoid prosecution. None of his crimes were uncovered.

Susan 'reprogrammed' all the other M series robots. They could no longer become 'rogue robots' on the Space Plantarium irrespective of who became 'Mission Controller.'

Susan was appointed as Professor of Botany.

Jude passed her finals with first class honours.

In the following years, Jude would often stand in her garden at night looking at the moon.

The survival of Wild Nature on planet Earth was precarious. Jude, and many colleagues in Botany, had begun to change the way plants were regarded and treated. She hoped that one day, the Plantarium could return to Earth and regenerate the natural world. She still had difficulty believing the journey she had made so far.